Ho-Ho-Hopeless Santa

For my very own elves, Lois and Joe — RG
For Mum and Dad, with love — SJ

SIMON AND SCHUSTER
First published in Great Britain in 2016 by Simon and Schuster UK Ltd
1st Floor, 222 Gray's Inn Road, London WC1X 8HB
A CBS Company

A CIP catalogue record for this book is available from the British Library upon request

ISBN: 978-1-47117-822-1
eBook ISBN: 978-1-4711-4601-5

Printed in China
2 4 6 8 10 9 7 5 3 1

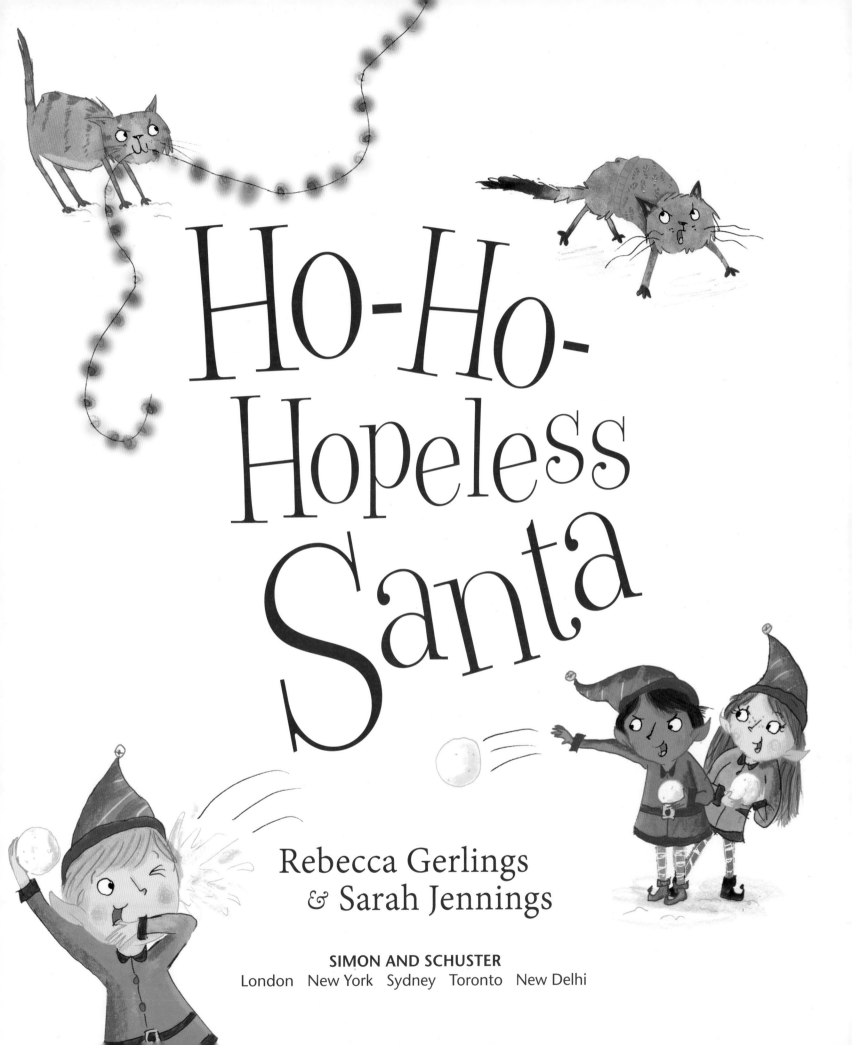

Ho-Ho-Hopeless Santa

Rebecca Gerlings
& Sarah Jennings

SIMON AND SCHUSTER
London   New York   Sydney   Toronto   New Delhi

It's Christmas time,
and up in homes go stockings,
trees and cards.
   While inside Santa's workshop
all the elves are working hard.

They glue and paint and pack the gifts;
their pile grows ever higher.

And even though they work long hours
they never seem to tire . . .

But spreading Christmas joy is not as easy as it seems . . .
The floor is getting sticky;
ribbons tangle round the beams.

The wrapping paper's running out;
the workshop's in a state!
For the very first time ever,
it seems Christmas might be late!

And what's caused all this kerfuffle?
It seems Santa's lost his list!
In all his years of Christmas
not a present has been missed.

The elves tell Santa,
"Take a break! We'll sort this muddle out!"

So Santa grabs a little nap,
while they all rush about.

At last, the sleigh is loaded up,
and Santa gives a wave.
But the magic isn't happening;
the reindeer won't behave!

It takes some elves – in total twelve –
to get them all in line.
With a heave and a ho, away they go,
it's gift-delivery time!

Up Santa soars, high in the sky,
he knows it top to bottom.

But – uh-oh –
something's going wrong,
it looks like he's forgotten!

He swerves to miss a pylon,
then he knocks a chimney pot.

He bumps into a lamp post,
and he gives some trees
the chop!

Down skids the sleigh – phew! – on safe ground,
it slides to its first stop.
Then a string of twinkly fairy lights
gets Santa on the hop.

He goes to press the doorbell,
but remembers just in time!
He throws the sack onto his back,
and then begins to climb . . .

Come on, Santa, let's get moving,
there is no time for slacking.
Those stockings can't just fill themselves.
Hurry up! We must get cracking!

Oops! Be careful! Mind that tree!
And don't tread on the cat!

Quickly eat up that mince pie
and what's that on your hat?

When dogs nip Santa's bottom – ouch!
He can't help but yell out loud.

But his magic works on tricky pets –
no biting is allowed!

The final house he visits is
the best you've ever seen.
With turrets, columns, and a flag,
it looks fit for a queen . . .

Santa's work is almost done.
At last, he's feeling calm.
Until the sleigh lands with a bump . . .

And sets off an alarm!

Guards appear from left and right,
the intruders are in trouble!
Then everyone's confused –
could it be they're seeing double?

Riding bareback on a reindeer,
is another man in red.
Yes, Santa One is an imposter,
here's the real Santa instead!

"We were only trying to help!
Sorry, Santa!" the elves cry.
Real Santa rolls his eyes and smiles
"Not bad for your first try!

But now there's lots of work to do.
No time to hang about!
So, go Team Christmas – HO, HO, HO!
Let's sort this muddle out!"

First they switch the royals' gifts –
Real Santa brought replacements.

Then round the world
Team Christmas zooms,
from tower blocks to basements.

Real Santa has a new list,
electronic (to save paper).

It makes fixing things so easy,
they've soon circled the equator.

The elves track their snowy footprints,
to remember where they went.
All the chimney pots now straightened?
Tick! Each lamp post now unbent.

Decorations back up on trees?
Tick! Everyone asleep? Tick!
All the presents are unjumbled,
just like magic, double-quick.

With everything just as it should be,
Christmas Day begins to dawn.
Back to Lapland, elves and Santa,
"Yes, we did it!" they all yawn.

So watch out this year on Christmas Eve,
should things at home be funny.
And do double-check your Santa,
in case elves are in his tummy!